Other Books About
Calvin Coconut

TROUBLE MAGNET

THE ZIPPY FIX

DOG HEAVEN

ZOO BREATH

HERO OF HAWAII

KUNG FOOEY

MAN TRIP

Calvin Coconut

ROCKET RIDE

Calvin Coconut

ROCKET RIDE

Graham Salisbury

illustrated by
Jacqueline Rogers

WENDY LAMB BOOKS

Visit us on the Web! randomhouse.com/kids
Educators and librarians, for a variety of teaching tools, visit us at
RHTeachersLibrarians.com

Library of Congress Cataloging-in-Publication Data
Salisbury, Graham.
Calvin Coconut : Rocket ride / by Graham Salisbury ; illustrations by Jacqueline Rogers. — 1st ed.
p. cm.
Summary: New fears for fourth-grader Calvin include a school bully named Tito and the return of his estranged father, rock star Little Johnny Coconut.
ISBN 978-0-385-73965-8 (trade) — ISBN 978-0-385-90799-6 (lib. bdg.)
ISBN 978-0-375-89798-6 (ebook) — ISBN 978-0-375-86508-4 (pbk.)
[1. Bullies–Fiction. 2. Fathers–Fiction. 3. Schools–Fiction. 4. Hawaii–Fiction.]
I. Rogers, Jacqueline, ill. II. Title. III. Title: Rocket ride.
PZ7.S15225Cadp 2012
[Fic]–dc23
2011043612

Printed in the United States of America

10 9 8 7 6 5 4 3 2 1

First Edition

For Joey and Takako,
my good buds . . .
and for Barbara Perris,
who for years has helped make me
a better writer.
Thank you!
—G.S.

For Benjamin
—J.R.

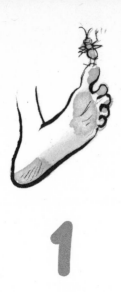

1

Hamajang

Boy, was everything all hamajang.

That means totally mixed up.

It was a hot Sunday afternoon, and I was sitting in a shady grove of ironwood trees at Kailua Beach Park watching an ant crawl over my toe. I thought of squishing it, but my friend Julio once said if you're mean and kill a bug you could come back in your next life as a bug yourself, and someone could squish you!

Scoot, ant. I don't want to get squished.

"Probably you don't either, huh?" I looked up to see if anyone was around to hear me talking to an ant.

Luckily, no one was.

I brushed the ant away with my finger.

Down in the small waves that slapped up on the beach a bazillion kids were shrieking in the sun.

My little sister, Darci, was one of them.

But not me.

Because everything was hamajang.

My *dad* was coming to town!

In less than two weeks!

Mom had told me and Darci about it the night before. She'd just heard about it herself.

None of us had seen Dad since he and Mom split up four years ago. He'd moved away, gotten married again, and was a rock-and-roll entertainer in Las Vegas, Nevada. The last time I saw him was at the airport. He was carrying his guitar case, with LITTLE JOHNNY COCONUT painted on it in silver. He knelt down and looked at me. "I'm going to see you often, Calvin. Count on it."

"Okay." It was all I could think of.

"I love you, son."

Then he was gone.

That was four years ago. We hadn't seen him since. He did call once in a while, and he sent stuff, like birthday presents and postcards. But we hadn't seen him.

Now he was heading to Honolulu with his band—Little Johnny Coconut, touring with his new CD, *Rocket Ride.* Dad had made sure Hawaii was on the schedule because he wanted to see us.

And I was scared.

There.

I said it.

Sure, I was excited, too, and I wanted to see him like crazy. I couldn't think of anything else.

But suddenly I had all these questions.

What was he like now? What was his new wife, Marissa, like? Would he still like me? Would she like me? What would I say to him? What would he say to me . . . or Darci . . . or Mom?

Jeese.

"Calvin!" Darci shouted from down by the water. "Catch!"

I grabbed my Styrofoam bodyboard and held it up just as the hard sand ball she'd made hit with a thunk.

She plopped back down and dug up more wet sand to start building another one. She probably wasn't worrying about seeing

Dad. She was only three when he left. How much could she even remember?

It was different for me. I could remember lots. Like how quiet our house was after we got back from the airport, and for weeks after that. Mom tried to smile a lot, but you could tell she was thinking about stuff.

After a few months it got better. Mom met Ledward, and Dad did call us once in a while. So we all sort of figured it out.

I stood and headed down to the water. The ocean was as warm as a bathtub.

Mom was at work, selling jewelry at Macy's in Honolulu.

So Stella took us to the beach.

Stella was sixteen and lived with us as Mom's helper. She didn't

like the beach because she burned easily. But today she'd invited her boyfriend, Clarence, to come along. "Watch your sister," Stella said to me, slapping sunscreen on Darci's cheeks, then her own.

She tossed the sunscreen to me.

Darci went back to digging in the sand, and Stella headed down the beach with Clarence.

Another sand ball came flying in and whacked my back, followed by Darci's shriek of laughter.

"Got you!"

"Yeah, you did, you little pest."

She ran up to me. "Make one, Calvin, and throw it at me."

I half-laughed. "Naah. No fun."

"No fun? You make the best sand balls of anyone."

"Aren't you thinking about Dad coming to town, Darce?"

She shrugged. "No."

"Well, I am, and I can't *stop* thinking."

"Why?"

"I don't know. But . . . he's coming." Just saying that made my stomach get butterflies.

Darci smoothed the sand ball with her hands. "He's kind of famous now."

"Yeah."

"I like his new song. It was on the radio."

"It was?"

"Stella heard it and came to get me. You weren't home."

Small waves ran up over my feet and sucked sand out from under them when they went back out. Coming and going. Like Dad. Anyway, I couldn't believe he had another song on the radio. Wow.

"So, what do you think Marissa's like, Darce?"

"Nice. Probably."

"What do you think she looks like?"

Darci tilted her head. "Stella?"

"That would be unfortunate."

"Huh?"

"Nothing."

What *did* Marissa look like? I'd seen a picture of her once, but she was really small in it. She and Dad were at a lake in some desert. There weren't any trees around.

Darci sat and started making a sand castle, so I took my bodyboard into the water and caught a couple of waves. But it wasn't much fun, so I went back into the grove of trees.

When Stella wandered back with Clarence, she

stopped and looked at me. "Why aren't you in the water?"

I shrugged.

Clarence smiled at me. He was a really big guy, a senior at Kailua High School. "He's thinking about his pop," he said.

Stella looked back at me. "Is that right, Stump?"

"Don't call me Stump!"

"Well, *are* you?"

I shrugged. "Maybe."

Stella's face was as red as a boiled lobster. Too much sun.

She humphed. "He calls you, doesn't he?"

"Yeah."

"So what's the big deal?"

She grabbed Clarence's hand and pulled him up to where their stuff was. She glanced over her shoulder, as if she wanted to say more, but didn't.

The next day at school my hamajang life got worse.

2

The Incident

Even as kids were still pouring off the school buses, a crowd was growing behind the cafeteria. Something big was up.

I ran over and elbowed in next to my friends Julio, Willy, Rubin, and Maya.

"What's going on?" I whispered to Julio.

"Tito was teasing Shayla."

"Why?"

"Shhh. Watch. Lovey's mad."

Lovey Martino, a sixth grader, was standing in the middle of the crowd, face to face with Tito Sinbad Andrade, the biggest, toughest kid in school. Tito's two friends, Frankie Diamond and Bozo, were watching, looking amused.

"Lovey's mad about Shayla?"

"Shhh!"

Shayla sat next to me in Mr. Purdy's class. Tito never bothered with fourth-grade girls. Yet Shayla was hiding behind Lovey with tears running down her cheeks.

"Ho," I whispered. I'd never seen Shayla cry. It made me feel bad.

Lovey stood inches from Tito. Her hands were balled into fists, and she was squinting up at him.

"Little lady," Tito said, grinning down at her. "You know you're the love of my life, right?"

"Yeah, well, you're the *creep* of mine."

Frankie Diamond spurted out a laugh.

Most of the guys in school looked like mice next to Tito. They felt like mice, too. Tito, Frankie Diamond, and Bozo were all sixth graders, and sixth graders ruled Kailua El.

Lovey poked Tito's chest with a finger. "What are you, *Sinbad,* some kind of big boy or something? Is that what you think you are? Listen to this: *Leave that girl alone.*"

Ho! She knew his middle name and *used* it! If we did that he'd grind us into cat food and stuff us in a can.

Tito held up his hands. "Me? What I did?"

"You know what you did, you big bully. You made fun of her shirt. Look at her. She's crying."

Tito glanced at Shayla. "So?"

"So *this,*" Lovey said, raising her fist. "Next time you mess with her I got a knuckle sandwich for you. *Pow!*"

Tito turned to Frankie and Bozo. "Look how much she loves me."

Lovey spat in the dirt. "Yeah . . . like I love boogers under my desk."

Frankie Diamond cracked up.

Tito grinned while Shayla wiped her tears with the palm of her hand. Dumb Tito.

Then I saw it. Oh no—

Shayla was wearing a Little Johnny Coconut T-shirt.

That's what Tito was teasing her about?

Did she wear that shirt to school because of *me?* I knew she liked me, but . . .

I didn't want to know.

"Look at that shirt," Tito said, pointing to Shayla. "Stupit. Little Johnny Coconut's music stinks."

Hey! I thought.

Lovey didn't budge.

Julio, Willy, Rubin, and Maya all turned to look at me.

I squinted at Tito, mad. But I kept my mouth shut. I didn't want to get in trouble.

Lovey poked Tito again. "If she likes it she can wear it. And I like that shirt, too. What do you think about that, fool?"

"I think maybe you and me go beach, ah? Bring some soda pops and have a picnic."

Lovey shoved him. "Go back under your rock."

Lovey put her arm around Shayla and they headed toward the classrooms.

"Wow," Maya whispered. "Go, Lovey!"

Tito turned to glare at us. "Whatchoo punks looking at?"

Like cock-a-roaches, we ran.

3

Mouse

My desk was by the window in the front row. Shayla sat next to me on the right. Almost always she drew weird pictures of toads or bothered me with questions before our teacher, Mr. Purdy, got started.

But now she sat staring at her desk with her Little Johnny Coconut T-shirt turned inside out.

I felt like a slug. I should have said something, like Lovey did. What Tito did was mean, and I wanted to tell Shayla that I liked her shirt, and that I should have stood up to Tito, too.

But I sat at my desk like the silent coward I was.

Dumb Tito.

"I guess you saw what happened before the bell," Shayla said without looking at me.

"What? Oh . . . uh, yeah."

"I'm sorry he said what he did about your dad's music."

I looked at Shayla.

"It doesn't stink," she added, glancing over at me. "I like it."

I nodded. "Uh . . ."

What a mouse. I couldn't even stand up for my own dad's music.

"I'm really sorry I wore this shirt, Calvin. I didn't mean to embarrass you."

Embarrass *me*?

"That's all right," I mumbled.

"No, it's not."

I frowned at the terrarium on Mr. Purdy's desk, which was right in front of me. Manly Stanley, our class pet centipede, was squinting at me, like, *If you think you're a coward I have news for you—you are.*

I looked at my desk. Someone before me had gouged *Mickey Mouse* into the wood.

That's what I was. A mouse.

When I looked up, even Manly Stanley had turned his back on me.

Later, at lunch, I was sitting across from Julio, Willy, and Rubin in the cafeteria when something wet hit the back of my neck.

"Ack!" I reached back to touch it.

It was white bread soaked in water, or at least I hoped it was water, not spit. I turned around.

Tito spread his hands as if to say, *I didn't do it.*

Right.

"Dumb Tito," I mumbled. I wiped my neck with my napkin. "Watch him, okay? Tell me if he's getting ready to throw something again."

"Okay, but—"

Another piece of wet bread hit my head.

"Cut it out, Tito!"

I stood and shook it from my hair. So *gross.*

"Cut it out, Tito," Bozo echoed in a squeaky voice. What was he, Tito's parrot?

"I'm out of here," I said, picking up my lunch tray. "See you guys outside."

Julio, Willy, and Rubin got up with me.

"Cut it out, Tito," Bozo squeaked again as we headed over to dump our trays.

Dingbat.

We went out to the schoolyard. The sun felt good.

"Why's he suddenly a bigger idiot than usual?" Julio said.

I shrugged. "Maybe he's flunking sixth grade."

"Never," Julio said. "You think his teacher wants him in her class for another year?"

"Good point."

We found some shade under a tree and sat.

"I wanna go for a rocket ride, / This stupid song makes my brain cells die," Tito sang, strolling our way with his dumb friends.

"He's got brain cells?" Julio said, low.

A laugh burst from my mouth.

"Rocket Ride" was my dad's new song. And those weren't the words.

"Leave us alone, Tito," I said, trying to look serious.

"Why?"

"Because I said so."

Jeese! Why'd I say *that*?

I felt my friends tense up.

"Well, now." Tito squatted down next to me. "Because you said so?"

He looked up at Bozo. "What should I do about this?"

"Take um out back and school um."

Tito nodded.

Frankie Diamond shook his head. "Come on, Tito. Leave them alone. They just little guys."

Tito turned back to me. "You need to get schooled, Coco-punk?"

"Uh . . . no."

"Huh."

Bozo grinned, showing his crooked teeth.

"Bozo thinks you do." Tito stood. "Let's go. Get up."

I didn't move.

"He doesn't have to," Julio said, getting up.

Thank you, Julio!

"Yeah? Well, guess what. I going school the both of you." Tito stared at Willy and Rubin. "Should I make it four?"

Willy frowned. "Guess so."

"Yeah, me too," Rubin said.

"Ha!" Frankie Diamond coughed. "The little bugs got guts!"

Tito glared at us.

I stopped breathing.

Then he broke out his big grin. "Little dudes, how can I beat you up? Like Frankie said, you got guts, and you gotta respect that. Who needs trouble with the principal, anyways? Bye, stinkbugs."

They slouched away.

I didn't have guts.

But my friends sure did.

"Thanks for standing up for me, guys. I lost my mind there for a second."

Julio grinned. "I didn't stand up for you. I stood up to *run*."

I shoved him and we laughed. "You punk," I said.

4

Bulldozing Rice

After school I got Darci from her first-grade classroom and started to walk home.

Julio, Willy, Rubin, and Maya waited for us in the field behind the school, like always, but I told them to go on without us. "I have to ask Mr. Purdy something."

"We can wait," Maya said.

"No-no, go home. I'll catch up."

That wasn't true, but I just didn't feel like talking.

"Come on," I said to Darci, heading over to my classroom.

But before we got there I stopped and looked back. My friends were out of sight, so I turned around and headed home again—only slowly so we wouldn't catch up.

Darci tugged on my arm. "Don't you have to ask your teacher something?"

"No. I just made that up."

"Why?"

"I didn't feel like talking."

"Oh."

We walked all the way home in silence. Darci was a good sister. I could always count on her.

My dog, Streak, came out of the garage wagging her tail. I squatted down to scratch her ears.

"Thanks, Darce," I said, looking up. "I just needed some time to think."

"That's all right. I was thinking, too."

"You were?"

"Sure. I always think. Don't you?"

"Were you thinking about Dad?"

"No. Was I supposed to?"

"Uh . . . no . . . just curious."

Darci smiled and headed into the house. How could she be so calm? My brain was like an anthill somebody kicked.

I stood up. "Come on, Streak."

We went into my room, which was made from half the garage. Streak hopped onto my lower bunk. I climbed up top and sat with my bow, shooting suction-cup-tipped arrows at my closet door until I got bored.

That night Mom's boyfriend, Ledward, came over to grill lime chicken and asparagus on the hibachi. Mom made brown rice and cut up some oranges.

Normally I'd have been saying, Ho man! Let's eat!

But I sat bulldozing rice around my plate with my fork. I felt like a stinky wet towel somebody left on the bathroom floor.

Mom reached over and touched my arm.

"What's bothering you, Cal?" Her voice was soft and my throat choked up.

"I'm okay, Mom," I squeaked.

The phone rang and Stella jumped up to answer it. "This is Stella," she sang sweetly.

She listened for a moment, put the phone against her shoulder, and looked at Mom. "It's your ex."

Mom gave Ledward a quick glance, got up, and took the phone into the kitchen. But we could all still hear.

"Johnny?"
Dad.

Mom mostly listened. The conversation lasted about five minutes.

"All right, yeah, great," she said. "I'll tell them right now."

Mom said goodbye and sat back down at the table.

She looked at Darci, then me.

"What?" I said.

"That was your dad calling from Los Angeles. He has a concert there this weekend. After that, he and Marissa will fly to Honolulu a couple of days earlier than planned. He wants to spend a whole day with us. All of us." She glanced at Ledward.

Finally Darci got excited. "When, Mom, when?"

"Next week, Wednesday. You get to skip school."

5

Johnny at the Concert Hall

It's amazing how fast your mood can change. One second I'm a stinky wet towel and the next I'm a rocket to the moon.

Ho yeah!

"His concert is next Saturday in Honolulu," Mom went on. "At the Blaisdell Concert Hall."

"The *big* concert hall?"

Mom smiled. "Looks like his fame is growing."

"Ho," I whispered.

The concert hall was where the big-time events took place.

"It's his Rocket Ride tour," Mom went on. "They're performing in twenty-five cities across the U.S. They just added the Honolulu stop, which is why we're only hearing about it now."

My stomach felt jittery.

"'Rocket Ride,'" Ledward said. "His new song?"

Stella nodded. "It's actually good."

I gaped at Stella. She hardly ever had anything nice to say about anything.

"What are *you* looking at, Stump?"

I blinked. "A toad?"

Her eyes narrowed.

"Calvin," Mom said.

"She started it."

"Nobody started anything. Finish your dinner. We're making s'mores over the hibachi after you do the dishes."

"After *I* do the dishes?"

"One day you'll be out there living on your own, and doing dishes is a handy skill to have."

Stella winked. "Your very first skill."

"Fine," I said. I'd show her my skill . . . at eating s'mores.

Mom tapped the table lightly. "Oh, one more thing, Cal. Your dad is giving us ten tickets for front-row seats. You and Darci can each have five. You two decide what to do with them, and Led and I will figure out a way to get everyone there."

"Really?"

"Yep. Exciting, isn't it?"

"Can I invite Stella and Clarence?" Darci asked.

"Of course you can, sweetie."

"I invite you, Ledward," I said.

Darci jumped up. "And I invite you, Mom!"

Mom and Ledward grinned at each other. "Well, thank you," Mom said. "Both of you."

Darci counted on her fingers. "I have one extra, Calvin. You can have it."

"Thanks!"

I counted tickets on my own fingers. Now I had six. Take out two for me and Ledward and that left four. I pushed my chair back. "Can I be excused? I'm going to call Willy, Julio, Rubin, and Maya. That's who I'm inviting."

"Sure," Mom said. "You can call right after you do the dishes."

I called Maya first. "I'm in," she said. "And Calvin?"

"Yeah."

"Thank you for being my friend."

"Uh . . . sure."

Rubin was next.

"Oh man," he said. "That would be so cool! But I can't. It's my cousin's birthday. We're going night fishing with his dad. But hey, thanks anyway."

Julio was next.

"Awesome!" he said.

Then Willy.

"Hot dang! I've never been to a concert. *Thanks,* Calvin!"

So—me, Ledward, Julio, Willy, and Maya. That left one ticket.

Streak followed me into my room and jumped up on the lower bunk. I slid in next to her. "Who should I invite, Streak? I have one ticket left."

She licked my cheek. She was the best dog ever. Who cared if her breath smelled like dead fish?

"So what do you think?"

Streak woofed. She wanted to play, not think.

"Okay, okay."

I leaned over and looked under the bed for her slime-crusted, smelly old stuffed hedgehog. "There it is."

Just as I grabbed it, a little voice in my head spoke up.

Shayla.

I looked up. What?

You know she's a big Little Johnny Coconut fan. Invite her. She has that T-shirt, remember. Be generous. Give her that last ticket. If anyone deserves it, she does.

"Shhhh! Shuddup!" I'm not giving my last ticket to Shayla. She's a pest, she's annoying, she's nosy, she's a know-it-all. And that's that!

Woof!

Streak grabbed the hedgehog out of my hand and jumped off the bed, ready to play.

You know she's the one.

No, no, no!

"Come on, Streak. Let's get out of here!"

Shayla, I'm telling you!

6

Tickets

Before school on Tuesday, word was spreading like the smell of frying bacon—Little Johnny Coconut was coming to Honolulu!

Darci and I were instantly famous . . . which sort of wasn't really a good thing.

"Heyyy, Coco-friend, Coco-pal, my buddy, howzit? You need anything, jus' ask and I get

you um." Tito put his arm around my shoulders. "I heard your daddy was coming to town."

He pulled me away, giving Julio and Willy stink looks.

Tito smiled at me. "Listen, Coco-friend, you know what I said about your daddy's music? I was just fooling. You know that, right? I like Little Johnny Coconut songs. For real."

I glanced back at Julio. He stuffed a laugh, and that almost made me crack up.

Not a good idea.

You punk, Julio! I tried to keep a straight face. Cut it out!

Tito tipped his head toward Julio. "Whatchoo looking at him for, ah? He just a cock-a-roach. Come hang out wit' me and Frankie. Bozo, too, when he gets here. He kine of slow."

"Uh . . . I have to—"

"Sit with us till school start. No bell yet."

I frowned.

Tito pushed me. "Come. I got something for show you."

Rubin was practically on the ground laughing. Maya put her hands on her hips and glared.

I made a face at them. *Help!*

Tito and Frankie Diamond took me to the tree no one else in school would even think of getting close to.

Tito reached into his baggy shorts pocket. "Look what I got."

He grinned and held up Dad's new CD.

"Can you get him to sign it for me?"

"Well . . . I guess."

Tito grinned. "Here. Take um. Bring um back later. It's good music. Ah, but you already know that, right?"

I took the CD, still in its wrap. He probably got it the minute he learned my dad was coming to town just so he could get it autographed and sell it for double afterwards.

Tito pulled out a pack of gum and offered me one.

I shook my head. "Mr. Purdy will just make me spit it out."

"I was in that boot camp, too. You know that?"

"No."

"Yeah, me and him, we got along fine. Was okay, that class. I got good grades."

"You did?"

"Yeah."

"You know what Tito wants, don't you?" Frankie said.

I shook my head.

"A ticket to your daddy's concert."

Tito snapped his fingers. "Hey, good idea! Whatchoo think, Coco-pal? You can get me one? And how's about for Frankie and Bozo, too? Us, we like that music, ah, Frankie?"

"Yeah-yeah, sure. Whatever."

I looked away. Think of something to get out of this mess!

Tito slapped my back. "Whatchoo say? You got tickets, right?"

"I only have one left."

"Yeah-yeah, but you can get more, right? Your daddy ain't going turn you down."

I frowned.

"Figure it out," he added, grinning like a crook in a bank vault. "We counting on you, little ticket man."

Talking to a Centipede

The next morning Julio and Willy helped me sneak past Tito. I hid in our classroom until school started.

"He won't find you here," Julio said.

"I hope not, because guess what?"

"What?"

"My dad's concert is sold out. We heard that last night."

"Wow," Willy said. "Awesome."

Julio humphed. "Yeah . . . awesome until Tito finds out there's no more tickets."

Later, when the morning recess bell rang, the room cleared out fast, including Mr. Purdy.

But I sat at my desk gazing out the window. No way I could go outside and not be bugged by Tito.

I frowned and got up to check in with Manly Stanley, lounging on the sand in his terrarium.

"You got any advice for me, Manly?"

Manly looked up, like, Sure, you want to borrow my stinger?

"Yeah! Good one, Manly!"

I half-laughed.

I jumped when someone said, "Are you talking to Manly Stanley, Calvin?"

Shayla.

"What? No . . . I mean . . ."

Shayla started digging through her desk.

I watched her a moment. "What are you doing?"

"Looking for something I drew. How come you're not outside?"

"Uh . . . I had . . . um, some homework to finish."

Shayla stopped digging and looked up. "Did we have homework?"

"No-no, it was . . . old homework. Yeah, old."

She had on her Little Johnny Coconut T-shirt again, this time right side out.

"Why'd you wear that shirt again?"

"Lovey said I should wear it and not let Tito bully me out of it. I'm going to wear it *until* the concert . . . and *to* the concert."

My spirits jumped. "You got a *ticket*?"

"No, but my mom said she'd take me. She's getting tickets."

Aiy.

"Here," she said, pulling something out of her desk. "You want it?"

She handed me a drawing of a toad wearing a cowboy hat. It was smiling, and a tooth sparkled with rays that shot out from it.

Good grief.

"Uh . . ."

"Keep it. I have more. Want me to draw you one with a guitar? Like a Little Johnny Coconut toad?"

"What?"

"Or maybe I could draw you a dog one, for your dog. What's its name?"

"Streak."

I looked at the toad in the cowboy hat. How does she think of this stuff?

"You like it?" she asked.

What I like is privacy. Go away! "Yeah, sure. It's fine . . . but why a cowboy?"

"I like to be creative. Mr. Purdy says creative people make the world more interesting.

Maybe when I'm at the concert I'll draw something."

"Um . . . about that concert."

"What?"

I clammed up. Let her mom break the news. Why should I be the one to tell Shayla that the concert was already sold out? "Well . . . uh . . . I hope your mom can get those tickets. It might be kind of hard."

"Oh, my mom knows how. I'm so excited to see him! You have a famous dad, Calvin. You're really lucky!"

I looked away. "Uh, yeah, I guess."

"See you there."

There was a long moment of silence. I looked at the clock.

Shayla said, "You are going, aren't you?"

"Going where?"

"The *concert*."

"Of course I'm going. He's my dad."

She started singing. *"I wanna go on a rocket ride, / Past the moon and out the other side."*

Get me *out* of here!

"Do you think he'll sign my CD if I take it?"

I glanced at Manly Stanley. Help me! You have to!

Your mess, not mine, Manly said.

"Uh, yeah . . . sure, Shayla," I said.

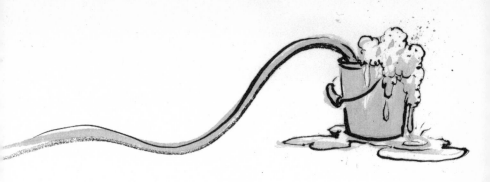

8

A Promise is a Promise

That Saturday Mom backed the car out of the garage and said she'd give me five dollars if I washed and vacuumed it.

Five dollars! Easy money!

"Sure, Mom. For two dollars more I'll wax it, too? Clarence taught me how."

Clarence was very particular about his car.

45

If he found even a tiny scratch he was all over it, buffing it out or painting it with a miniature paintbrush.

"Wash and vacuum is fine, Cal. But thank you for offering. Maybe next time."

So I was out in the driveway with Streak, a hose, and a big fat sponge when Tito, Frankie Diamond, and Bozo showed up.

Great.

I went over and turned off the water.

Streak ran up to them, her tail wagging. Good guys, bad guys—she liked them all.

Frankie Diamond dropped to a crouch. Streak went right to him and nosed his out-stretched hand. "Yeah, you happy to see Frankie, ah?"

Frankie looked up at Tito. "Dogs can tell when somebody likes them."

Tito wasn't interested.

"You like me help you wash that car, Coco-hose?"

"Naah. I got it."

Tito shrugged. "We was just going down to

the beach and I thought, you know, maybe we stop by and see if you snagged me that ticket yet. I mean, only got a week till the party."

"Party?"

"Yeah, the one we going have at your daddy's concert."

I got down on my knees and started scrubbing a wheel. "No, I don't have—"

"Man, I like that Little Johnny Coconut song 'Rocket Ride.' It's *cooool,* I tell you. Am I right, Bozo?"

"Maybe to you, Tito, but to me it stinks."

"How 'bout you, Coco-hose?" Tito said, standing over me. "You like your daddy's new song?"

"Yeah. It's good."

Tito crouched down and said in a low voice, "Not much time for get me that ticket. You going get me um, right? You promised."

"What? I never—"

Tito held up a hand and stood. "A promise is a promise, ah? Laters, Coco-man."

"I didn't promise!"

But Tito, Frankie, and Bozo were already walking away.

Later that day, I was walking with Julio on the golf course that was just beyond the jungle that edged our neighborhood. The fairway was empty. And safe. No golfers or greenskeepers in sight.

"You promised him?" Julio asked.

"No, I never promised anything. He just made that up!"

"Typical. Listen, forget Tito. Don't give him anything."

"And die."

"He's all talk. Shut him off like a radio."

"Easy for you to say."

We heard a jeep engine and turned to look back.

Beep! Beeeeep!
We sprinted
into the jungle.

I could hear the
jeep racing toward us.
It belonged to the golf
course, and riding in it
were two greenskeepers,
the golf course police.
They loved chasing kids
off the fairways.

We sank into the jungle
shadows as they slowly
cruised past, looking into
the bushes.

The jeep stopped.

We crawled into a thicket of weeds and crunched down in it.

One guy got out and walked right by us.

"You see um?" the driver asked.

"Nope. Lousy kids. I get my hands on them they going know it."

The guy in the jeep said, "Come on, Jimmy. You were a kid once yourself, remember?"

"Yeah, but I obeyed the rules."

"Sure you did." The driver laughed, shaking his head. "Come on, get in. We got work to do."

After they drove off, Julio and I crept back out onto the fairway.

"I got an idea," Julio said. "You give that last ticket to the guy Clarence, and tell Tito to get it from him."

"Ha!"

Julio grinned. "Does Tito know that Clarence is Lovey's brother?"

"I don't know, but there's one problem . . . Darci already invited Clarence."

"Hmmm. You're still in trouble, then."

9

Bazookalolo Weird

On Monday at school I was sitting in the shade with Julio, Willy, Rubin, and Maya. "Help me, guys," I begged. "How can I get Tito off my back?"

Julio gave me a sad look. "Yeah, we're really going to miss you."

"What?"

"After he murders you. We'll be sad for a whole day."

Julio cracked up.

"Hi, Calvin," someone said, and I looked up.

Shayla smiled and waved as she walked past with a girl named Michelle.

I lifted my chin. Man, can't she leave me alone for one second?

"Ooo," Rubin whispered. "Somebody likes somebody."

"Shuddup," I mumbled. Shayla was so embarrassing.

"Shayla's nice," Maya said. "Right, Willy?"

"Uh, yeah, nice. I think."

I frowned. "Nice like a mosquito singing in your ear. I wish she'd just leave me alone!"

Julio made a kissy face.

"Seriously, guys. Forget Shayla, I need help!"

"Okay," Julio said. "Here's what you do with Tito . . . give him that ticket."

Maya shoved him and he fell over. "Calvin's not giving that creep anything."

Julio sat back up. "Watch out who you're pushing, girl."

Maya threatened to push him again.

I folded my arms over my knees and frowned.

Give it to Shayla. Solve your problem.

Dang voice!

Do it.

I puffed up my cheeks and let the air out slowly.

Be a man.

All right!

I picked up a pebble and threw it. Hard. "I'm *not* giving it to Tito!"

"Now you're talking," Maya said.

"I'm giving it to . . . Shayla."

Everyone looked at me. *"What?"* Rubin said.

Maya smiled. "That's nice, Calvin, really, really nice. Shayla! Why didn't I think of that?"

I clenched my jaw, determined. "Shayla honestly likes my dad's music. Tito prob'ly wants to go just so he can say he went. But Shayla should be the one, because she got teased, and I didn't even stand up for her." I shook my head. "I owe her. Only Lovey did anything to help her, and Shayla is one of us, even if she is a pest."

Willy, Julio, and Rubin gaped at me.

"I'm not changing my mind."

"But what about Tito?" Willy said.

"I'm not scared of him."

I wasn't. I was terrified. But I'd stood up to Tito before and I could do it again.

Good job, the little voice said.

I stood up. "Got to find Shayla before I change my mind."

Maya sprang to her feet. "I'll help you."

Julio, Willy, and Rubin looked up, their mouths hanging open. I couldn't blame them. I was being bazookalolo weird, but so what? Sometimes Shayla was an annoying know-it-all who drew dumb toads and wouldn't leave me alone . . . but she wasn't a bad person.

I was doing the right thing. For once.

Attaboy.

10

We're Going to
Miss You

Maya and I found Shayla sitting on a bench with Michelle. They were talking, their knees all pointed toward each other.

We started toward them, but stopped.

"What?" Maya said.

"I can't do this with Michelle there."

"Why not?"

"Well, she'll think I like Shayla."

"No she won't."

"I'm outta here."

Maya grabbed my shirt and pulled me back. "No. What you're doing is good, Calvin. Don't stop now."

I crossed my arms. "Not until she's alone."

Maya turned toward Shayla. "Wait here."

Oh man, I thought.

Shayla and Michelle looked up as Maya approached. Maya said something and pointed toward the school office. Michelle popped up and headed off.

Maya gave her a small wave and walked back toward me.

"All yours," she whispered.

"What do I do?" I whispered back.

"Invite her!"

I puffed out my cheeks and headed over.

Shayla smiled. "Hi, Calvin."

"Hey," I said, casual-like. Just passing by.

"Where's your friends?"

I looked toward them. "Over there."

They waved, grinning.

Man, was I going to get them!

I turned back to Shayla. "Say . . . listen, I wanted to, um . . ."

"Do you want to sit down?"

"Uh . . . no thanks. I just wanted to tell you something."

Shayla smiled. "Okay."

She was making this too hard. Why couldn't she just be nosy or bratty or something so I could just walk away and forget it?

"I, um . . . Well, you see, my dad gave me some tickets to his Rocket Ride concert and—"

"Oh, you lucky! My mom tried to get tickets and they were all sold out. Did you know that? That means he's extra, extra popular. That concert is going to be sooo *goooood*!"

"Uh, yeah, well . . . I thought . . . I wondered . . . Well, I'm inviting Julio, Willy, and Maya to go with me, and—"

"Oh, Calvin, that's so nice of you!"

"Yeah, Well, listen. You can come, too . . . if you want. I have one more ticket."

Shayla looked at me, speechless for the first time ever. In her whole entire life.

Then she spouted, *"Eeeeeeeeeee-yes!"*

She leaped up and threw her arms around my neck. She hugged me so hard I nearly fell over. "Thank you! Thank you! *Thank! You!*"

I wiggled free.

Everyone within a hundred miles was looking at us. A wave of heat burned my face. Julio, Willy, and Rubin were rolling on the ground holding their stomachs.

I felt like throwing up.

Shayla grabbed my hands and squeezed. "You are the nicest person in the world, Calvin! I've got to tell Michelle."

"But . . ."

She let go and ran off.

Julio, Willy, and Rubin shrieked with laughter, and Maya tried to get them to shut up.

I stormed over to them. "Stop! Laughing!"

"All right, all right," Willy said, falling back on the ground.

"Everyone is looking at us!"

"It's okay, Calvin," Maya said. "No one cares."

I dropped down next to Maya and sat with my knees up, glaring at the ground between my feet. "What did you say to Michelle?"

"I said the principal wanted to see her."

I looked at her, like, Serious?

Maya shrugged. "She'll get over it."

Rubin nudged me with his foot. "I can't believe you did it."

"Yeah," I said.

"But you have one more thing to do."

"What?"

He pointed with his chin. "Tell him you just gave his ticket away."

I turned and saw Tito looking over at me. He waved.

"Great," I mumbled.

"For sure, we're going to miss you."

11

Scarfing the Cone

On Tuesday I started getting this crawly feeling in my stomach. The next day we were going to Honolulu to see Dad and Marissa. Why do I feel like this? I thought. He's my *dad*!

I needed to turn off my brain.

But how?

That night Ledward showed up with two containers of ice cream. We made cones and took them out onto the patio. Except for Stella, who was on the phone with Clarence in the kitchen.

I held up my cone as I headed out. "Yum."

Stella waved me away with the back of her hand.

I made a kissy face and left.

It was almost full dark outside. The trees were shadowy silhouettes against a cloudless gray sky, and stars were just beginning to pop out. Except for Stella, it was a nice night.

I bit into my monster chocolate cone. Already it was melting. In Hawaii you couldn't take forever with ice cream.

Mom looked at me. "You ready to see your dad again, Cal?"

"I guess."

She nodded. "I know it's hard."

"It's okay, Mom. It's just kind of weird."

"I know. It's weird for me, too." She pulled two plastic patio chairs together. "Here. Sit."

I sat.

Ledward slapped his neck. "Mosquitoes. What do you say we go inside, Darci?"

Darci grabbed his hand and they left.

"So," Mom said, facing me. "Tell me how you *really* feel."

I sat down. My ice cream cone was starting to drip.

"I don't know," I finally said. "Like when you get butterflies in your stomach?"

Mom waited, then said, "Do you *want* to see him?"

I looked up. "Well . . . sure. It's just that I don't even know if . . ." I shook my head. "My brain just won't stop, Mom. I keep thinking stuff like, Will he look the same? Will he like me? And what about Marissa? Will she like us? I just want to stop thinking, that's all. I can't even sleep. It's sort of . . . scary."

Mom looked into my eyes.

I could hear Ledward and Darci talking in the kitchen, and Chris Botti's peaceful trumpet drifting out from Stella's window.

"It's completely normal to feel that way, Calvin," Mom said. "What you're thinking shows how much you care, and that's a good thing, a real good thing."

"It is?"

"It is, and you'll feel a thousand times better when you actually see him. Everything will be fine, and all those thoughts will go away, I promise. Do you remember when he used to take you out in your red skiff?"

I laughed. "Yeah. He was a terrible rower." I could picture him sweating, his black hair shiny in the sun and the silver St. Christopher medal he always wore stuck to his chest.

"And he would complain that the boat wasn't made right and that he should have gotten you a kayak instead?"

"Or a canoe."

"And then you both would laugh about it later."

I nodded. "Yeah, I remember."

"So does he, Calvin. I promise you, he hasn't forgotten a minute of it. Your dad loves you just as much now as he did back then."

I looked down. We did use to have a good time.

She smiled. "Better work on that cone. It's all over your hand."

I licked my wrist and scarfed the cone the way Ledward did, biting it.

Mom reached out and put her hand on my shoulder. "Hey . . . remember that man trip you took with Ledward?"

"Yeah."

Ledward had taken me fishing on the Big Island with his friend Baja Bill. I would never forget the giant marlin that charged our boat!

"You tagged a marlin," Mom went on. "By yourself. You even reached out and touched it, remember?"

"Yeah, that was amazing."

"Ledward and I learned something about you from that trip."

"You did?"

Mom smiled and sat back. "Uh-huh. We learned that you have courage, Calvin. You're going to be just fine when you see your dad. I know that for a fact."

12

Little Johnny Coconut

Wednesday.

The time had come. I was going to see my dad for the first time in four years. Funny thing, I was more excited-nervous than nervous-nervous.

Stella stayed home from school, too, so she could come with us. When Ledward pulled up in his jeep, we were waiting, all dressed up and ready.

We piled into Mom's car and headed over the mountains to Honolulu. Ledward drove.

When we'd just passed through the tunnel at the top of the mountain, Stella reached across Darci and handed me a folded note.

I looked at it, then at Stella. "What's this?"

She'd turned away.

I opened the note.

A small photograph fell out. It was a picture of a young guy standing by a horse. He was about twenty years old and wore a cowboy hat that seemed way too big. A good-looking cowboy staring at the camera, like a movie star.

"Who's this?" I said to Stella.

She ignored me, looking out the window.

I picked up the note.

This is my dad.
He was a professional rodeo bull rider
until he broke his back. He got fixed up and

wasn't paralyzed, but he could never ride a bull again. After that he changed. He became dark and violent, and my mom left him, taking me with her. I was five. I haven't seen him since. I don't know where he is, and he doesn't seem to be looking for me. Just wanted you to know that you aren't the only one with a dad who took off. It happens. I don't feel bad about it. I just wish I could see him once or twice. This picture is what I wanted to show you. At least you get to see your dad. Get it?

I studied the picture again, then folded it back in the note and handed it over to Stella. She took it and looked at me.

I nodded and whispered, "Got it."

She gave me a little smile.

A half hour later we pulled up to the entrance of a big, fancy hotel. A man dressed in a white uniform opened the door for Mom.

She spread her arms. "This is just lovely."

Ledward gave the car keys to another guy, who drove the car away.

Whoa, I thought, looking around. This place is awesome!

I'd been to Waikiki once before when Mom and Ledward had taken us to climb to the top of Diamond Head. But I'd never been to *any* hotel.

We headed into an open lobby. You could look right through it to a fishpond with colorful carp in it, and birds on rocks around the edges. A giant turquoise swimming pool was beyond that, and then the beach and sparkling blue ocean.

Ho!

"Can we go swimming now, Mom?" Darci asked. We'd brought our suits. Dad had told Mom there were four pools, or we could go to the beach if we wanted.

"Let's wait a minute, Darci. But soon, okay?"

Darci knelt over the fishpond, looking at the orange-and-white carp. "Look! Real fish!"

Mom and Ledward gazed out over the pool to the ocean.

Stella sighed. "Someday I am going to stay here for a week."

Darci looked up. "Where's Dad, Mom?"

"Well, he said he'd meet us here in the lobby." She looked at her watch. "Right about now."

"Dad," I whispered as he headed toward us.

He looked smaller than I remembered. But he had that same crooked smile he got when we used to talk about my red skiff. He was squished between two of the biggest guys I'd ever seen in my life, way bigger than Ledward.

Ho, my dad needs *bodyguards*?

Dad waved.

Behind him a lady hurried to catch up. Marissa? She wasn't how Darci and I had pictured her at all.

She was tall and had kind of wild blond hair, and lots of bracelets on her arms and rings on her fingers. Big round hoops hung from her ears, and she carried a purse big enough for Streak to take a nap in. She walked funny, on elevator shoes made out of cork.

Dad opened his arms. "Calvin! Darci!"

Darci hesitated, then ran to him.

I didn't budge. He looked like some man I only sort of knew one time, not my dad. It was weird.

People stopped to gawk at him but didn't come too close. I heard a kid say, "Mom, Mom, is that Little Johnny Coconut?"

The mother pulled a camera out of her purse.

Dad picked Darci up and swung her around, then set her down and hugged her close. "It's so good to *see* you. Look at how you've grown!"

After a moment, he let Darci go and hugged me, too.

"Hi, Dad," I said.

"Good grief, Calvin, I've sure missed you."

"Yeah," I said.

He wore cowboy boots and jeans with holes in them, the kind you buy that way if you're rich. His shirt was bright blue, the color of sailboat canvas. He still wore the silver St. Christopher medal around his neck.

I wanted to say something . . . but what?

Dad pushed me away. "Look at you. You're nine feet tall!"

I glanced at Mom.

Stella, Ledward, and the fancy woman stood watching.

Dad put his arm around my shoulder. "We've got a lot of catching up to do. I want to

74

hear all about what you've been doing, every-thing, you hear?"

"Sure."

"Good, good."

Mom reached out to shake hands with the fancy woman. "Welcome to the islands. I'm Angela. And you must be Marissa."

The woman laughed. "Oh, heavens, no, I'm Rachel, Johnny's manager. Wherever he goes, I go. His life is getting more hectic these days, what with 'Rocket Ride' climbing the charts."

"Well, it's nice to meet you, Rachel."

Mom turned to Dad. "Good to see you, Johnny. You're looking well."

"You are too, Angie. It's been a while, hasn't it?"

"Yes, it has."

They gave each other a quick hug; then Mom turned to Ledward. "Rachel, Johnny, this is my good friend, Ledward Young. He was nice enough to drive us over here this morning."

Ledward gave a slight bow to Rachel, then reached out to shake hands with Dad, who was shorter. "Very happy to meet you, Johnny. I've heard a lot about you."

"I hope it's all good."

"It is, for sure. By the way, congratulations on 'Rocket Ride.' It's a great song and I hope it goes all the way to the top."

"Well, that makes two of us."

There was a moment of silence.

Then Dad said, "Oh, Rachel, do you have those tickets?"

"Right here."

Rachel pulled an envelope out of her huge

purse and handed it to Mom. "Ten front-row seats just for you!"

"Let me see!" Darci jumped up to grab at them, but Mom hid them away in her purse. "Later, sweetie, okay?"

"Okay, fine, but can we go swimming now?"

"Soon."

"Where's Marissa, Dad?" I wanted to meet her, to see what she looked like.

He glanced out toward the pool.

"She's going to meet us over there at the beach bar. She just got out of the water. She loves the ocean, you know. Rachel has a section reserved where we can sit right by the beach."

"Little Johnny!" somebody called.

Dad waved.

He turned back to us. "Privacy is a bit hard for me to come by these days."

"Don't let him fool you," Rachel said. "He loves it."

We walked down past the one-legged pink flamingos, the fishponds, and the big blue pool to the beach bar. Rachel chatted with curious people along the way. We sat in a roped-off area around a couple of tables, looking out over the bright sand to the calm sea.

Wow, I thought. It's like we're with the president of the United States or something.

"Look at the water," I said. "It's so smooth!"

Ledward leaned close. "This side of the island is sheltered from the wind. We live on the windward side, which means–"

"We get all the wind."

"You got it."

I snapped my fingers. "*That's* why all the sailboarders and windsurfers come to Kailua!"

"Yup." Ledward ruffled my hair with his big hand.

Dad studied us with a half smile. "So," he said.

We waited for him to say more, but he just smiled.

"Why don't you tell us about your tour, Johnny?" Mom said.

That seemed to come as a relief to Dad. "Well . . . I never thought my life would get this frantic, but I guess that's what . . . you know . . . what success does."

He looked up and waved. "Over here!"

A huge smile crossed his face. "And this, folks, is my Marissa."

"Ho," I whispered.

Marissa

Marissa could have stepped right out of a magazine. She had long brown hair and wore white shorts, a yellow tank top, and thin leather sandals on her tanned feet.

She came to me first and looked into my eyes. "Without question, you are Calvin. I see Johnny all over you. Am I right?"

"Uh . . . yeah. That's . . . me."

"You are every bit as handsome as your father."

I must have looked like a cow standing there with my mouth open.

She hugged me, then crouched down to look Darci in the eye, too. "And you are Darci, every bit as beautiful as your mother."

"Thank you," Darci squeaked.

Right away I could tell Marissa was special. It was her eyes! They were light blue, like when there's no wind and the ocean looks like glass. You just stare at it, thinking, Wow. Her eyes were like that. And when they focused on me, I felt like she really, really liked me.

I glanced at Mom.

Did she see this, too?

Mom smiled.

Marissa winked at Darci, then stood and turned to Mom. "And you're Angela."

"Yes." Mom reached out to shake Marissa's hand. "I'm so happy to finally meet you, Marissa."

Marissa smiled. "Me too. And to be honest, I thought this moment would be awkward. I was so nervous that I . . . well, for one thing, I spilled orange juice all over the table at breakfast."

Dad laughed. "And in my lap."

Marissa grabbed his hand. "But you know what?" she said. "Right now I feel . . . well, like we've been friends for years. I don't know why I was so bumbly about all this."

Mom stepped forward and gave Marissa a hug. "Welcome to the other half of your family, Marissa."

They hugged again.

Marissa wiped a tear from her eye.

Amazingly, so did Stella.

While Mom and Ledward talked to Dad and Marissa at the beach bar, Darci and I went swimming. It was fun running back and forth between the big blue pool and the beach.

"Come swimming!" Darci shouted to Stella, who was lounging by the pool with a book.

Stella smiled and waved her off.

Darci and I plopped down into the small waves that slapped up onto the sand.

"What do you think of Marissa, Darce?"

"She's nice. I like her."

"Yeah, me too. Do you wish Mom and Dad were still together?"

Darci shrugged.

"Yeah, I know what you mean," I said. "It's sort of okay like it is, isn't it?"

"Uh-huh, because we have Ledward and Stella now, too."

"Stella! Are you crazy?"

"I like Stella."

"I like her, too . . . like I like scorpions."

"Because she calls you Stump?"

That started a water war.

A while later, Dad walked down to us. "You two want to go for a walk with me and Marissa?"

"Yeah!" we said at the same time.

So, along with the two silent giants who followed at a distance, we headed down the beach.

"Why do you have bodyguards, Dad?" I whispered.

"To tell the truth, I don't know. I'm not that famous, for sure! The bodyguards were Rachel's idea."

"Johnny had a small problem at one of his concerts," Marissa said. "A fan got a little too . . . friendly."

"Huh?"

Marissa laughed. "Okay, this woman jumped up onstage and ran over to Johnny and hugged him right in the middle of a song. Security had to rush in and take her away. It was innocent, but it got Rachel worried. What if some violent person did that? So now Johnny has bodyguards."

"Wow," Darci said.

"Wow is right," Marissa agreed.

I glanced back at the giants. I was glad they were there, even if they didn't smile or speak.

Dad put a hand on my shoulder. "You know, Calvin . . . I was so . . . anxious about seeing you and Darci. I haven't been an on-the-job kind of dad. In fact, I've been pretty terrible, and I'm so sorry about that."

I kind of nodded. I didn't know what to say.

Marissa took my hand.

Dad smiled. "From now on things will get better. I promise. I can't tell you how much being away from you eats at me."

Marissa grabbed Darci's hand, too. "But that's all going to change."

Dad reached over and gave me a quick hug. It felt good. "You know, now that things are working out well for me, I'll be able to fly you and Darci over to Las Vegas. Would you like to come stay with me and Marissa sometime?"

I looked at him. "You mean . . . fly by ourselves? Just me and Darci?"

"No, I'd come get you."

That was a relief. "Well, in that case, yes!"

"How about you, Darci?" Dad asked.

"Can I bring Stella?"

"Sure you can," Marissa said. "Everyone who wants to come is welcome in our house. It's not that big, but we'll make room."

Why had I felt so nervous about all of this? Dad still *liked* us.

And so did Marissa.

There was only one thing left that I really wanted to know: What was Dad like when he became Little Johnny Coconut?

14

A Good Day to Die

The next day during morning recess I hid
from Tito in the bushes. Everything about the
concert was all figured out . . . except for Tito.
All I had to do was hide from him for two
more days.

Julio, Rubin, and Willy helped me keep
watch.

Willy tapped my arm. "Look."

I peeked through the weeds. "Aiy."

Tito, Bozo, and Frankie Diamond were strolling our way.

"He knows we're here," Julio whispered.

"How? He can't see us."

"Trust me. He's going to walk up like nothing is going on, and then when he's close, he's going to pounce on you."

"I'm outta here."

"Me too," Rubin said.

We all eased back into the bushes.

"Uh-oh," Julio said. "Here they come. Run!"

We took off and ran around the cafeteria to the front of the school. We slid to a stop. Where to go, where to go?

"The library!"

We sprinted across open ground to the library. I prayed Mr. Tanaka, the librarian, wasn't there. He might just kick us out.

"Well, well," Mr. Tanaka said, looking up as we burst through the doorway. He was on a stool with his guitar. "Come on in, boys. I was just showing these kids how to write a song."

A big group of second graders sat around him on the carpet. All of them turned to gawk as we slipped into nearby chairs. I glanced over my shoulder at the door.

No one there.

"Do you know who these boys are?" Mr. Tanaka asked the second graders.

They shook their heads, no.

"Well. These boys are here to help us write songs today."

Wait. What?

Mr. Tanaka looked past us toward the door.

Tito, Bozo, and Frankie Diamond stood at the entrance to the library, probably for the first time in their lives.

Mr. Tanaka turned to me and raised his eyebrows.

I opened my hands as if to say, If you kick us out I'm dead, Mr. Tanaka.

Mr. Tanaka said, "Come on in, boys. The more the merrier."

They came in and sat behind us.

Mr. Tanaka picked up his guitar. He had lots of instruments in his library. He was a librarian, but he also played in a band.

He strummed a chord and looked out over the group. "Who knows who Little Johnny Coconut is?"

Almost every hand went up. "'Rocket Ride!'"

Someone else shouted, "A singer!"

Mr. Tanaka strummed a chord again. "Correct! Who knows who that boy is right there?"

He pointed at me.

"That, my young songwriters, is Little Johnny Coconut's son, Calvin. He goes to our school."

In one tick of the library clock, I became famous.

I slid down in my seat.

"Come up here, Calvin."

Great. He was making me pay for interrupting his class.

"Sit."

I pulled a stool over and sat next to him, facing the second graders. I looked at Tito, waiting for him to smirk.

But he didn't.

"Your dad writes his own music, right?"

"Yeah. I guess."

"Did he ever show you how to write a song?"

"No."

"Well, it's not so hard. Here. I'll strum two chords and you think of a melody, and maybe some words if they come to you."

"Me?"

"Why not?"

Mr. Tanaka strummed one chord for a short while, changed to another, then went back to the first.

Tito leaned forward, listening.

Mr. Tanaka strummed the chords again. The only song I could think of was the Starship Troopers song "It's a Good Day to Die."

I sang, *"Uh, look out the window and see that big blue sky, / It's so hot on the road you could watch a fried egg fry."*

The second graders laughed.

I sang more.

"So you'd have to agree, uh . . ."

I looked at Tito.

"Uh, you'd have to agree it's not a good day to die."

"Dumb!" Bozo shouted.

Mr. Tanaka held up his hand. "Cork it, Bozo. Remember where you are."

"Yeah, sure, Mr. T., but that's just dumb words he made up."

"All songs begin with an idea, Bozo, and Calvin's idea was about what a nice day it is. Am I right, Calvin?"

"Exactly, Mr. Tanaka, it's a nice day to be alive."

Man, did I want to get out of there!

Tito said, "That was pretty good, Coco-dude. Keep going."

Huh?

Mr. Tanaka jumped in. "See, class, see how it works? We're starting to get somewhere. Calvin had an idea, and Tito liked it. We have a song started."

The second graders nodded.

"Tito," Mr. Tanaka said. "I've heard you play before. Come on up here and take this guitar."

Tito grinned and got up. "My uncle taught me. But only slack key."

Slack key was Hawaiian music played on a guitar that was tuned different than regular.

Tito sat, tweaked the tuning, and started to play.

My jaw dropped. Tito played like someone on the radio. He was good!

"Wow," Willy whispered.

"No kidding," I said.

When Tito finished, everyone clapped, loud and long.

He gave the guitar back to Mr. Tanaka. "Sorry, Mr. T. Got kine of carried away."

"Anytime, Mr. Andrade. Anytime."

"Someday I going play in a hotel. That's what I want."

Tito suddenly kissed his fingertips and blew the kiss to someone in the back of the room.

Lovey Martino was standing in the doorway.

"That song was for you," Tito said.

Lovey humphed. "Not bad."

"I knew it. She loves me."

Tito looked at me. "Maybe someday I might be famous like your daddy."

I had to agree.

Me and my friends headed back to class, still amazed at what we'd just heard.

15

Big Fat Mess

Tito caught me in the cafeteria at lunch.

"Heyyy, little bug, you know you can't hide from me." He put his arm over my shoulder. "Outside. We fine a place to talk."

I glanced around for help.

Julio, Willy, and Rubin kept their gaze on their trays.

Tito scoffed. "How come you looking at them, Coco-moco? They not going help you. Anyways, you just going give me that ticket. We out of time."

Tito and I went out into the sun.

"Uh, listen, Tito . . . I don't, you know . . . like . . . have any tickets? I gave them all away."

"Huh. That's too bad . . . for somebody. So what ticket you going give to me? And how's about one for Frankie?"

"I'm telling you, I don't even have one."

Tito nodded. "Yeah. But do you get what I saying? Come on. The bell going ring soon. Give me um."

He reached out and wiggled his fingers.

I looked at him. "Didn't you hear what I said?"

"Yeah. But that's your problem, right?"

"No."

He squeezed my neck. "What?"

I crunched up my shoulders. His grip was like giant pliers.

"'Kay, okay," I said. "I'll get one. One! That's all."

Tito patted my back. "Fine. Frankie don't care, anyway. When?"

"Tomorrow."

I rubbed the back of my neck.

Tito clapped his hands, grinning big. "I going bring my binoculars. I like to see um up close. Go."

Tito gave me a shove.

What a big fat mess.

In class I could hardly listen to anything Mr. Purdy was saying.

Think, think, think.

Break the problem down.

Okay. Number one, Shayla isn't my good friend. Number two, she isn't my family. Number three, sometimes I don't even like her very much. Number four, if I don't give Tito a ticket he could cause trouble for me *and* my friends. And number five, Shayla won't complain.

I don't like where this is going, the little voice said.

What else can I do? What else!

I scowled at the floor. Under Mr. Purdy's desk, a dead roach lay on its back with its feet in the air.

That afternoon as I was walking home from school with Darci and my friends, I stopped cold.

Julio looked back.

"Why'd you stop?"

"I have to do something."

"What?"

I turned back toward school. "Darci, walk home with Maya. Tell Stella I'll be home soon."

"Where are you going?" Darci asked.

I didn't answer. My fingers were trembling. Do it! Just do it, do it, do it!

You can't, the little voice said. *It's not right.* Shhh.

16

Shayla's Place

I sort of knew where Shayla lived. Maya had told me. It was an old building about a mile past the school, called Paradise Village.

Out on the street in front of the apartment building, five boys from the middle school were shooting hoops into a loop with no net. I had to walk by them to get to Shayla's apartment.

The kid with the ball looked at me and passed it, missing its mark on purpose. The ball bounced toward me.

I stopped it with my foot and picked it up.

Five sets of eyes locked on me.

I tossed the ball back and one guy caught it, never taking his eyes off me.

Nobody moved.

"Who are you?" the guy with the ball asked.

Dang.

"Uh . . . um . . . a friend of someone who lives here?"

Dumb. It sounded like a question.

"Yeah? Who?"

"A girl. Uh . . . Shayla?"

Four of the five guys laughed and shoved the one kid who didn't. He glared at me. "Whatchoo want with her?"

"I have . . . just something to tell her. We're in the same class at school."

"I'll tell her, what is it?"

Ho, now what? "I need to tell her myself."

"Melvin," someone called. "Leave him alone. He's my friend."

Me and the kid, Melvin, glanced up to the outside walkway that ran by the doors on the second floor. Shayla waved at me. "Calvin! What are you *doing* here?"

"I came to . . . to talk to you."

"Well, come on up."

Melvin shrugged and tossed the ball to another kid.

I headed up the stairs.

Shayla waited at the railing outside her door. "This is so weird, I mean, to see you here."

The door to her apartment was open and I glanced inside. It was a small place with one couch and a couple of chairs. No pictures on the walls, but there was a mirror.

"Want to come in? We have some guava juice."

"No, that's okay. I have to get home, you know, so my mom doesn't worry."

Shayla smiled. "Okay. What did you want to talk about?"

Yeah, genius, the little voice said. *Let's hear it.*

I looked over the railing, down at the guys shooting hoops. Melvin kept glancing up at us. This was going to be harder than I'd thought.

"Well, you know how I said you could go to the concert with us and—"

"Yes! And I can't wait!"

"Uh . . . well . . . um, something's, um, something's changed."

"Oh?"

"Yeah, well, you see, I don't have enough tickets for everyone, and . . . I mean . . . I mean—"

"What, Calvin?"

Man, this was hard. "You can't go."

Shayla looked at me, into my eyes, into my brain.

"Oh," she said. She blinked, fast, and her face got pink.

"I . . . I'm sorry, but—"

She reached out and put her hand on my arm. "That's okay, Calvin. I understand. It's fine. I heard Mr. Tanaka is going to tape it, so I can see it in the library later."

You slug! the little voice said.

I studied my feet. "Yeah. Well. I'm sorry."

Shayla looked down on the boys below. "Melvin is my cousin."

I nodded.

"Those boys just look mean, but they're not."

"Yeah, well . . . I have to go now."

"I'll walk you to the corner."

"You don't have to."

"I know, but I want to."

I nodded.

We headed down the stairs and past the boys, who didn't even glance at us.

Out on the street, we stopped and looked back at the apartments. "Well," Shayla said with a sigh. "At least I got a new outfit from it."

"Outfit?"

"My mom bought me new clothes to wear to the concert."

"She did?"

"I'll wear them to school tomorrow."

"Okay. Well. I'm really sorry. See you."

I waved and took off. I wanted to get home. Fast. I wanted to forget this ever happened. I felt like a sick dog. I could feel it in my mouth, like sucking pennies.

"Bye, Calvin!"

I kept on going without looking back.

The little voice in my head was dead silent.

Say something, I thought! Call me stupid. Call me mean.

Nothing.

17

Speechless

"Hey!" Maya called when I got back on our street. "Watch where you're going."

I looked up. "Huh?"

She was sitting on her front lawn fixing the strap on her skateboard helmet. She pointed with her chin. Her fat cat, Zippy, was stretched out in the middle of the road, like always. I was about to step on him.

"What's wrong with you?" Maya asked. "You're acting really weird today. You didn't even tell us where you were going."

I blinked at her.

"See? You can't even talk."

"I can talk."

"Prove it."

"I don't feel like it. Anyway, I gotta go home."

I stepped over Zippy.

Maya popped up, put her helmet on, and jumped on her skateboard. She zoomed up to me. "Come on, Calvin. You can tell me."

I kept my mouth shut.

"I mean it," she said. "I won't tell anyone, if that's what you're worried about."

"I'm not worried about anything."

She kept circling me on her skateboard. When we were just past Julio's house, I felt so bad I had to get it out. "Okay!"

I stopped and bunched my lips. "I told Shayla she couldn't go to the concert."

"What?"

"You heard me."

She nodded. "I wish I *hadn't* heard you! So what you're saying is, you invited her . . . and now you uninvited her?"

I frowned.

"But . . ." Maya was speechless. She stopped skating, kicked her board up, and grabbed it.

"I had to," I said.

"Why?"

"Tito."

"You took Shayla's ticket away to give to *Tito*?"

"Well, what else could I do? He kept–"

"You had a choice, Calvin! And you made the wrong one."

Maya dropped her skateboard and headed back toward her house.

That night I told Mom I didn't feel good and went to my room early. I just wanted to be alone. Except Streak could come in, because she liked me even if I was a skunk sometimes.

I climbed up to my bunk and lay with my hands behind my head. Dumb Tito!

I felt Streak jump onto the bunk below me.

Mom came out a while later with a bowl of soup and some saltine crackers.

"Maybe this will make you feel better, Cal."

"Maybe," I mumbled.

"What's wrong? Is it your stomach?"

I nodded. "Yeah."

"Well, the soup will help if you can get it down. If it gets worse, you come in and see me, okay?"

"Yeah."

Mom left, closing the door quietly.

If I ever needed a dog it was then. Dogs don't blame you for doing stupid stuff.

I rolled over and looked down. "Hey."

Streak raised her head but didn't wag her tail.

Bad sign.

I rolled back and put my arm over my eyes. "Say something," I said to the little voice in my head.

Anything.

Down at the river, even the noisy toads were silent.

Well.

You know how sometimes when you have a problem, and you think about it just before you go to sleep at night? And then you wake up in the morning or maybe even in the middle of the night and you have a solution for that problem?

That's what happened to me.

I woke up the next day feeling like I got my first A in math, ever. Even the little voice in my head was back.

Not bad, it said.

Boy, did it feel good to hear that.

I got dressed and hurried into the house. Mom hadn't left for work yet. "Mom," I said, grabbing a bowl and a box of Grape-Nuts. "You think Dad's up yet? I need to call him."

She glanced at the clock. "It's kind of early, Cal."

"I know, but can I call him?"

"You can try. What do you need to talk about?"

"Something."

Mom laughed. "Something, huh? Okay, I'll give you some privacy."

When she left the kitchen I grabbed the scrap of paper Dad's hotel number was on and punched it in.

He was up.

"Dad. This is Calvin. I need to talk."

18

Ooo-La-La

Friday.

At school I was nervous, but not the kind of nervous you get when you're going to the dentist, or when you have to stand up in front of the class and talk about a project.

It was the excited kind.

I sat at my desk waiting for Mr. Purdy to

start class. My leg was bouncing. I tapped my fingers on the desktop. Everyone was in their seats, talking low, mumbling.

Shayla was sitting quietly, not even drawing pictures, like she almost always did. Just sitting there in her nice new clothes.

Do it! Go!

"Uh, Shayla?"

"Oh . . . hi, Calvin."

"Yeah, hi . . . uh . . . I . . . Well, you know how I came to your house yesterday?"

"And met Melvin."

"Yeah, and I was . . . you know, like sort of weird?"

She looked at me. "You weren't weird, Calvin. I was glad you came over."

"You were? Why?"

She shrugged. "I don't know."

"Uh, yeah, well, I . . . I . . ."

My fingers trembled. I'd never in my life felt good nervousness like that before. "Listen, Shayla . . ."

"What is it, Calvin?"

"Um . . . you want to go on a rocket ride?"

I couldn't believe how my hands were shaking.

Shayla cocked her head. "What do you mean?"

"My dad's concert."

She frowned. "But you said I couldn't."

"I know. I was wrong to do that. But I fixed it. I got a great idea and I fixed it."

"What do you mean?"

"I got us backstage passes."

"What?"

"For you and me. We can watch everything from onstage, closer than front-row seats, and we can see what goes on backstage. We'll be part of the band, almost. Dad said he'd love it if we did that, because he wanted me to see what he does, and how much it means to him."

Shayla looked at me with her mouth half open.

Then she yelped and covered her mouth.

But the yelp was so loud the whole entire class plus Mr. Purdy jumped.

She leaped up and yelped again; then she hugged me.

"Ooo-la-la," Julio called.

The whole class burst out laughing, even Mr. Purdy.

My trembling fingers balled up into fists as

I slipped away from Shayla and slid down into my seat. My face was hot as a fresh pancake.

"Shayla!" I whispered.

She sat down. "Sorry. I was just excited—"

"Shhh!" I hissed.

She nodded . . . with a grin.

"Anything you care to share with us, Shayla?" Mr. Purdy asked.

Even Shayla turned red. "No."

"How about you, Calvin?"

I shook my head and covered my face with my hands. I could never look at anyone in that class again for the rest of my whole entire life!

What a man, the little voice said. *What a hero!*

19

Lovey's Power

I still had a problem.

Tito.

Because even though now I really *did* have one ticket left, I was NOT going to give it to him.

But I had a solution.

First, I needed to find Lovey before Tito found me.

"Lovey!" I yelled when I saw her standing in the shade with her friends.

They all turned to look.

I ran over, glancing around. No Tito. So far, so good.

"Can I, uh, talk to you?"

"Sure. What's up? That doofus bothering you again?"

"Not yet."

She laughed. "Come. Let's walk. Look," she said, nodding toward Tito's tree. "There he is. See?"

"Yeah."

Tito was watching us. Bozo and Frankie Diamond were leaning back against the tree with their arms crossed. "They try so hard to look tough," Lovey said.

"So, what can I do for you?"

"A favor?"

"Like what?"

Lovey was nice to me because her brother was Clarence, Stella's boyfriend. And despite how big and scary Clarence looked, he always treated me like a brother.

"I need you to save my life."

Lovey spurted out a laugh. "That's a big favor. How can I do that?"

"It's like this. . . . I have one ticket left to my dad's concert tomorrow, and Tito wants it. He's been in my face about it every day. But I've been, you know, hiding out, because I don't want to give it to him. It's not right, the way he wants it. Like, forcing me. So . . . I want you to have it."

Lovey stopped walking and looked at me. "Me? Why? Won't that make it worse?"

"No. It will make it better. You see, you're the only one he can't complain about. Know what I mean? Because he likes you. He *has* to be glad I gave it to you . . . instead of him. See?"

She grinned. "You're a smart kid."

"Only if it works."

"It will work! Watch. Here he comes."

I stepped back, holding my breath.

Tito slouched up with his two shadows.

"Heyyy, Coco-man," he said. "I thought we was friends." He turned to Lovey and smiled. Still looking at her, he added, "You trying to steal my girlfriend, Coco-dude?"

"No! I was just—"

Lovey put her arm around my shoulder. "My friend Calvin just gave me your ticket."

"Wha-what?"

"You know," Lovey said, smiling. "The ticket to his dad's concert?"

Oh jeese.

Tito studied me. "What's she talking about?"

"I . . . well . . ."

I looked for somewhere to run.

"Sorry you can't go, Tito," Lovey said. "Really I am. I know how much you like Little Johnny Coconut."

"Me? I don't like that crummy music. Whatchoo talking?"

Lovey slapped her cheek in fake surprise. "Oh, I'm sorry. I thought you were bugging Calvin for a ticket. Am I wrong?"

Tito gave me a look that said, I'm going to eat you.

Lovey touched his arm. "You know what else Calvin told me?"

I turned to her. *What?* I didn't say anything else.

"He said since you play slack key so well, I should ask you to play for me. Will you play for me . . . Tito?"

Tito turned to me. "Coco-puff said that?"

Lovey smiled. "Sure did."

Boy, she was good.

Tito stood taller. "I play for you anytime. Forget that concert. I going give you one better one."

She grunted. "Don't get carried away, big boy."

The bell rang, and I glanced at Lovey, my eyes trying to say, Thank you!

She winked.

I took off. Lovey just might be the love of *my* life, too.

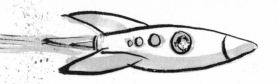

20

Rocket Ride

Saturday. Concert day.

The plan was that Shayla and I would meet a guy named Zeppo at the loading dock behind the concert hall, and he would take us backstage. He'd be wearing a red baseball cap with a yellow lightning bolt on the front.

"You can't miss him," Dad had said. "It's a one-of-a-kind hat."

"He'll give us passes?"

"He'll do better. He'll take you inside himself, past security and right to our dressing room."

"Wow," I'd whispered.

"And Calvin?"

"Yeah."

"I'm proud of you for doing this for that girl."

"You are?"

"Very much so."

Whatever bad feeling I had about everyone laughing at me at school and all that stuff . . . just flew out the door.

Poof!

We arrived in three cars—Mom's clunker, Ledward's jeep, and Clarence's big pink beast. Eleven of us. Since I now had a backstage pass,

Darci had used my ticket to invite her friend Reena.

"You and Shayla meet us right here when it's over," Mom said.

"Sure, Mom."

Ledward winked at me. "You two have a great time back there. What a treat that's going to be."

Mom looked at Shayla, all dressed up in her new outfit. "You look lovely, Shayla."

"Thank you, Mrs. Coconut."

"You sure you two can find this guy?"

"Yeah, Mom. Go on in. We'll be fine."

Mom gave Shayla a hug and kissed the top of my head, then went into the hall with Ledward and everyone else.

I grabbed Shayla's hand. "Come on! I don't want to miss anything."

As we ran around to the back, I realized what I'd done! I was holding hands! With *Shayla*!

I let go.

She grabbed my hand back.

Aiy.

We ran past two giant trucks parked by a closed roll-up door, leaped up some concrete stairs to a greasy platform, and banged on the first door we came to.

Bam! Bam! Bam!

I pounded again.

Finally some big guy opened it.

A *really* big guy. Huge like Dad's body-guards.

"Yeah?"

I gulped. The name *Zeppo* flew out of my brain. I couldn't remember it. "Uh . . . can I see . . . uh, Little Johnny Coconut? He's my dad."

"And I'm the tooth fairy, nice to meet you."

He started to close the door.

"No, wait! I'm Calvin, his son! I was supposed to meet someone here . . . a guy in a red hat. He has backstage passes for us."

The big guy looked down at me. "A red hat?"

"A baseball cap, with a yellow lightning bolt on the front. His name is—"

"Zeppo," the big guy said.

"*Yeah,* Zeppo. We're supposed to meet him here."

The big guy looked at me, then at Shayla. "Wait."

He closed the door.

Shayla grinned and raised crossed fingers.

The door opened and the guy in the red hat came out. "Man, I'm sorry. Just had a lot to do before they go on. Come on in. The warm-up band is playing now."

The music got louder and louder as we followed Zeppo down a long concrete hallway to stairs that took us up to a kind of waiting area.

Shayla grinned and covered her ears. "Awesome!" she shouted.

I could barely hear her, so I nodded.

We could see the warm-up band out onstage, and beyond them, the first few rows of seats. But everything past that was black because of the lights blasting onto the stage.

The music was so powerful that the beat went right into me, vibrating in my bones. It was impossible to stand still.

Shayla jumped to the rhythm next to me, and out in the audience people were standing and cheering and clapping and whistling. I looked for Mom.

Shayla pulled on my arm. "Calvin!"

I turned and saw Dad and his band heading toward their positions behind the curtain. He had his guitar strapped on, and his hair was sticking up all over the place to look wild and cool. He wore a black T-shirt and old jeans with silver-studded black boots.

I waved.

He gave me and Shayla a huge grin. "I

hope you like it, Shayla," he called. You had to read his lips, but it was clear what he said.

Shayla looked at me and mouthed, "He knows my *name*?"

"I told him," I mouthed back.

Shayla looked at me as her eyes filled with tears. But she had a big smile.

Ho man, did I say something wrong?

She wiped her eyes and turned back to the band, excited as a dog in a jeep.

Zeppo motioned us over to a better spot.

Now we could see everything on-stage and the people in the front three rows, including everyone we'd come with.

When the opening band hit their last notes, the crowd cheered even louder. The band jogged offstage, right past me and Shayla. They were dripping with sweat and grinning and saying stuff like "That was awesome!"

Then, while the crowd was still on its feet, a booming voice blared over the sound system. *"And now, straight from Las Vegas, Nevada, the band you've all been waiting for, the only mainland band with roots in Hawaii . . . give it up for Hawaii's own . . . Little! Johnny! Cohhh-cohhh-nut!"*

The place went bazookalolo!

That hall was as loud as all six Blue Angel fighter jets blasting low over your head.

Dad's drummer started hammering on his drums as the curtain rose.

Boom! Pok!

Boom-boom, pok!

Boom! Pok!

Boom-boom, pok!

The crowd went wild as the band started off with Dad's last big song, "I Love Sunshine Pop."

The concert hall was alive with everyone hooting and screaming. It was a song that was so easy to sing along with, and that's just what Shayla and I were doing.

"Dom, dom, dombie-do-dombie-dombie-do . . ."

Shayla grabbed my arm and squeezed.

Song after song, nonstop, the crowd stood and cheered and sang along, and when, two hours later, the concert ended with "Rocket Ride," the concert hall felt like some cool alien monster, rocking and rolling, totally wild.

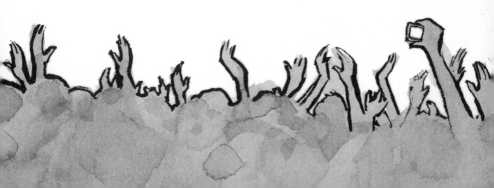

"I wanna go on a rocket ride,
Past the moon and out the other side.
Sailing through a billion diamond stars—
Call it crazy but you got to get away for a
    while."

Shayla knew all the words. We sang them as loud as we could. We jumped and danced and clapped, and when it was over we staggered from laughing so hard. It was so much fun I forgot all about Shayla being the pest from school.

"Calvin! This was the best concert *ever!*"

"Yeah. For me too, Shayla . . . me too."

21

Falling Star

At the end of the show the band left the stage, but the audience kept clapping and shouting and whistling and whooping.

Dad came up to us, his hair plastered with sweat. He ran his arm over his forehead and gave us a huge grin. "Hear that, Cal? They loved it!"

"Yeah! So did we, right, Shayla?"

"It was so, so *amazing!*"

"Well, hang on a minute, Shayla, because we're going back out there to do one more song, and I have something I want you two to do for me. You willing to help us out?"

"Yeah!" we both said.

"Zeppo!" he called. "The Frisbees."

Feet started stomping. The crowd wanted Little Johnny Coconut to come back out.

Zeppo ran over with two boxes of fluorescent-green Frisbees. He pulled one out. "Like it?"

Printed on it in dark blue was a coconut tree on a small island, and *Little Johnny Coconut's Rocket Ride Tour.*

"Yeah!" I said. "These are great! What are they for?"

"For you and Shayla to zing out into the audience during our last song. You watch . . . the place will go nuts!"

"You mean, go out *there*?"

"Piece of cake. You can do it."

I looked at Shayla.

She beamed.

Man, I was suddenly so nervous I thought I would faint. Go out there in front of all those *people*?

Zeppo handed us the boxes of Frisbees.

I looked at Dad. "So, we just throw them out there?"

"Spread them around. Try to get them all over so no section feels left out. Do your best." Dad grinned and called to his band. "Let's go!"

They jogged back onstage. The place roared like thunder in the mountains. So wild it gave me chills.

Little Johnny cranked on his guitar and let loose on a song called "Black Cadillac."

"Zip 'em!" Zeppo shouted, pushing us out from behind the curtain.

Shayla and I ran out with the boxes of Frisbees. Lights exploded in my eyes.

I couldn't see anything. I raised my hand to block the glare.

Little Johnny sang, *"I love my black Cadillac, my shiny Cadillac, yeah, just my buddies and me . . ."*

Shayla grabbed a handful of Frisbees and shoved a bunch at me. She ran to the other side of the stage. When the audience saw what we were about to do, everyone started leaping up and waving for us to throw the Frisbees their way.

Zing!

The first one I tossed went toward Darci. Stella caught it and gave it to her. Darci held it high, jumping up and down to the music.

Zing!

Zing!

Zing!

It was so much fun I couldn't even believe it. What had I been so nervous about? Shayla was zinging those Frisbees way out into the audience. She was dancing really good, too, almost like she was part of the show. It made me smile. Shayla was a rock-star dancer!

Ho!

"Black Cadillac" ended right after we tossed our last Frisbees. Perfect. Dad and the band took a bow and motioned for us to join them. Holy moley!

Shayla and I ran off the stage with the band.

It was absolutely the biggest thrill of my life.

"Wow," I said to Dad. "You do this every night?"

He laughed. "Not every night, but close. You two did great out there, I mean really, really great!"

Shayla and I looked at each other. She couldn't have smiled any bigger if she'd wanted to.

"Here," Dad said, handing his guitar pick to Shayla. It was green, like the Frisbees, with the coconut tree on it in blue. "Something to remind you of tonight."

Shayla squeezed it. "I'll never forget this, *ever!*"

Dad winked at me.

I could hear people talking and laughing as they slowly made their way out of the concert hall.

Dad and his band fell into some folding chairs. Zeppo tossed them ice-cold bottles of water.

Man, the sound of that crowd would stay with me for my whole entire life. And the sight of Shayla, squeezing that tiny guitar pick.

See? the little voice said. *See what you did?*

Yeah.

It was kind of like seeing a falling star.

One minute it's there, so surprising.

Then it's gone.

But deep inside, you know you'll never forget what you saw.

22

Tito's Gift

That night Little Johnny Coconut and his band had to catch a flight back to the mainland. We said goodbye backstage, after celebrating the great show.

Our time with Dad was running out.

Marissa crouched down to Darci while reaching over to take my hand. "I just can't wait to have you two come visit us in Las Vegas. Boy, do I have things to show you."

Darci and I hugged her.

Just before everyone left, Dad pulled me and Darci aside. "Listen, you two. I want you to know that I'm going to be a better father to you, and that's a promise. I've missed too much, and coming here has been a real wake-up call for me."

"You're already a good dad," I said. "We just don't get to see you."

He smiled and hugged us both. "That's going to change."

"Oh," I said, remembering. "Can you do one more thing?"

"Anything."

I pulled Tito's CD out of my pocket. "A kid at school wants your autograph."

"Sure."

Dad signed it and handed it back. Sometimes Tito could be okay, I guess.

"Bye, Dad."

He hugged me and Darci.

Then he was gone.

I cruised through Sunday in a daze.

Man oh man oh man.

When I went down to the beach with Willy and Julio, we were still talking about the concert. Willy said, "I can't believe Little Johnny Coconut is your dad."

I grunted. "Sometimes I can't, either. On that stage he was like nobody I'd ever seen before."

"Crazy wild!" Julio added.

"What was it like, up there with the band?" Willy asked.

"Flat-out unreal!"

The next morning at school as the buses were arriving, I was hanging out by the cafeteria with Julio when Bozo zipped up on his old one-speed bike. He skidded to a stop, spraying dirt all over our feet. He got off and locked his bike with a fat chain.

"Who's going to steal that junks?" Julio whispered.

That made me laugh.

Bozo looked up.

"Whatchoo laughing at? You just look in a mirror?"

He cackled at his own lame joke.

Then he got serious. "Answer me what I asked, punk." He put his hand on my chest. "Talk before I turn your face into a pancake."

"I wasn't laughing."

"I heard you."

"Okay, I was laughing, but not at you."

Bozo grabbed my shirt and pulled me up, his face about an inch from mine.

I struggled to get free.

"Hey, hey, hey," somebody behind me said. "Whatchoo doing to my friend? Let um go." Tito squeezed between me and Bozo.

"This punk was laughing at me," Bozo said.
"I going make him sorry."

"Let um go," Tito said.

"But he—"

"Let um go, I said."

Bozo pushed me away and let go. My shirt
was all wrinkled up.

Tito smoothed it out with his hand. "Bozo
kine of touchy sometimes. I mean, when

you look ugly as him you got to be touchy, ah?"

He barked out a laugh.

Bozo scowled.

I pulled Tito's CD out of my pocket. "I got it signed for you."

"Ho!" Tito held it up. "Cool!"

He put his arm around my shoulder and winked at my friends. "Lissen, little bugs. I going give you a gift. For all of this week, ev'ry day, ev'ry minute, here at Kailua El, nobody going bother you. I promise. So relax, ah? Just cruise."

Tito shook his head, smiling. "I owe you, Coco-rock-and-roller-dude, and when I owe, I pay."

"Owe me for what? The CD?"

"You brought me and Lovey together, and I not going forget that, no."

He thought Lovey *liked* him? Huh. Maybe she did.

Tito let me go and reached out his palm for me to slap it.

I hesitated, then slapped.

"There you go!" Tito said, and walked away with Bozo.

When they passed Lovey Martino, she gave Tito a nod, like, That was nice.

"Hey, Lovey," he called. "I going play slack key for you soon. We go beach, you and me. I bring my guitar. How's about it?"

Lovey rolled her eyes.

Tito spread out his hands and said to the whole schoolyard, "She loves me!"

Rubin and Julio cracked up.

I don't know why, but just then I thought of Shayla's guitar pick. It made me smile.

When the bell rang, we headed to Mr. Purdy's room.

"Hey, Manly," I said to our class centipede as I slid into my seat. "Wassup?"

Manly scurried toward me in his terrarium. So what's next, Calvin? he seemed to say. You humans put on a pretty good show.

The next Saturday Darci and I went to the beach, taking Darci's Rocket Ride Frisbee. While we were tossing it around, three second-grade boys came running up.

"Hi, Darci, can we throw it, too?" one kid asked.

Darci beamed, so I handed the Frisbee to the boy. "Sure."

I went up to sit in the shade of the iron-wood trees. I put my hands behind my head, leaned back, and looked out over all that calm blue ocean. Today things weren't hamajang.

Nope. Everything was darn near perfect.

A Hawaii Fact:

The Big Island of Hawaii is home to the world's biggest telescope. It's on the top of Mauna Kea. The Mauna Kea Observatory stands at an altitude of 13,796 feet.

A Calvin Fact:

Julio read somewhere that this is the most tongue-twisty thing you can say in English: "The sixth sick sheik's sixth sheep's sick." Ho! You can hardly even *think* it, let alone say it! Try it. I dare you.

Graham Salisbury is the author of seven other Calvin Coconut books: *Trouble Magnet, The Zippy Fix, Dog Heaven, Zoo Breath, Hero of Hawaii, Kung Fooey,* and *Man Trip,* as well as several novels for older readers, including the award-winning *Lord of the Deep, Blue Skin of the Sea, Under the Blood-Red Sun, Eyes of the Emperor, House of the Red Fish,* and *Night of the Howling Dogs.* Graham Salisbury grew up in Hawaii. Calvin Coconut and his friends attend the same school Graham did—Kailua Elementary School. Graham now lives in Portland, Oregon, with his family. Visit him on the Web at grahamsalisbury.com and calvincoconut.com.

To listen to Little Johnny Coconut sing songs from Rocket Ride, go to grahamsalisbury.com/music.

 Jacqueline Rogers has illustrated more than one hundred books for young readers over the past twenty-five years. She studied illustration at the Rhode Island School of Design. You can visit her at jacquelinerogers.com.